Happy Faces
by Alberta Orr

SCOTT, FORESMAN AND COMPANY • GLENVIEW, ILLINOIS
Dallas, Tex. • Oakland, N.J. • Palo Alto, Cal. • Tucker, Ga. • Brighton, England

ISBN 0-673-10615-2

Mr. Vara had a store.

He lived above the store.

The store was across the street from
the school.

The girls and boys went to the store
to buy candy, gum, and ice cream.

One day Mr. Vara fell off a ladder and broke his leg.

The next day the store was closed.

Miss Cruz told the girls and boys
about Mr. Vara.
They wanted to help him.

They made cards for him.

They brought books, puzzles, and
food for Mr. Vara.

Miss Cruz took the girls and boys
to see Mr. Vara.

They went across the street and
up the stairs.

They gave Mr. Vara the cards and books.

They put the puzzles on the table.

They put the food in the kitchen.

One boy watered Mr. Vara's flowers.

One girl fed the fish.

Two boys washed the dishes.

The girls and boys sang a song.
They sang "Put on a Happy Face."

Mr. Vara said, "Thank you.
I like your song.
I like your happy faces."

A girl said, "We like your
happy face too."

Mr. Vara said, "Write your names on
my cast.
I want to remember my happy day."

The girls and boys wrote their
names on Mr. Vara's cast.
Then they went back to school.

1. Why did the girls and boys
   help Mr. Vara?

2. Why did the girls and boys
   have happy faces?

3. Why did Mr. Vara have a happy face?

4. What are some other ways the girls
   and boys can help Mr. Vara?

5 6 7 8 9 10 11 12 13 14 15 16 17 18 19 20 21 22 23 24 25 RRD 91